Cowgirl Legends

From the Cowgirl Hall of Fame

Written by Kathy Lynn Wills and Virginia Artho

Introduction by Pam Minick and Jimmie Gibbs-Munroe

Foreword by Reba McEntire

GIBBS·SMITH
P
PUBLISHER

Salt Lake City

98 97 96   5 4 3 2 1

This is a Peregrine Smith Book, published by
Gibbs Smith, Publisher
P.O. Box 667, Layton, Utah 84041

Design by Warren Archer
Margaret Formby, Executive Director, National Cowgirl Hall of Fame and Western Heritage Center
Madge Baird, Editor
Gail Yngve, Associate Editor

Library of Congress Cataloging-in-Publication Data
Wills, Kathy Lynn.
Cowgirl legends from the Cowgirl Hall of Fame / Kathy Lynn Wills and Virginia Artho.
        p.   cm.
ISBN 0-87905-708-4 (paper)
1. Women in rodeos—United States—Biography. 2. Cowgirls—United States—Biography.
3. National Cowgirl Hall of Fame & Western Heritage Center. I. Artho, Virginia. II. Title.
GV1833.5.W55 1994
791.8 ' 4092 ' 2—dc20
[B]   94-12403
                                                                 CIP

Dedicated to all cowgirls everywhere.

A few of the pioneer rodeo cowgirls:
Rae Beach, Ruby Gobble, Thena Mae Farr, and Nancy Binford.

Contents

FOREWORD

Photo: Peter Nash

The life of a "Cowgirl" always intrigued, mesmerized, and fascinated me.

I grew up on an 8,000-acre cattle ranch in southeastern Oklahoma. But the first time I was thrown up on a horse and told to "get in the brush and find some yearlings," the idea of being something other than a "Cowgirl" *did* cross my mind.

But a "Cowgirl" I was, and a "Cowgirl" I still am.

I've known lots of cowgirls in my life. Rough, tough, fearless, and always with the biggest hearts I've ever known.

Whether they are in the arena, the corrals, or out in the pasture, they know what to do. And because they are women, they have to do it three times better than any man there, to prove themselves and to be accepted.

God Bless the Cowgirls. He made us, He knows our hearts. And I pray that He keeps us safe until He calls us Home.

Reba McEntire

9

ACKNOWLEDGMENTS

I would like to thank my mom and Lydia at the WPRA for their help.
Kathy Lynn Wills

Thank you to the flesh-and-blood cowgirls who entered my life,
so willing to share their stories and answer streams of questions.
Virginia Artho

INTRODUCTION

McClean Stevenson was substitute hosting for Johnny Carson a few years ago when a cowgirl appeared as a "Tonight Show" guest. As she walked onto the stage, McClean and Ed McMahon said in unison, "*You're* the cowgirl?!" They probably expected her to be strolling out bowlegged and chewing tobacco—a typical stereotype.

But the word *cowgirl* brings to mind a corral full of images, as there is no one way to define the complexity of the title:

A cowgirl may be a young 4-H or FFA member grooming her steer for the upcoming stock show where she dreams of the grand championship and selling her stock for enough money to put herself through college;

She could be the high school rodeo competitor, feeding calves and horses early each morning, and sharpening her roping skills well into the night;

Or a cowgirl might be the woman fixing fence, riding herd, helping a cow drop its calf, roping and branding cattle on her ranch . . . a homemaker, a mother;

A cowgirl can be any number of things, but one thing is for sure . . . a cowgirl is a free spirit.

With a whole history of these spunky women, who were the first cowgirls? We think they were the pioneer women—strong, tireless, dependable, and multi-talented. We've read that in addition to helping build her home and sew the clothes, a pioneer cowgirl might also milk a cow, fix dinner, and give birth—all in the same day! They were a tough breed, and this is a trait that has passed on through generations of cowgirls, especially those in the rodeos.

Mitzi Riley, daughter of famed pioneer cowgirl Tad Lucas, recalled the early days of rodeo. "In the '20s and '30s everyone rode on trains—we'd load the horses and off we'd go to Chicago, New York, and Philadelphia . . . There was such a camaraderie among the competitors, especially the women."

Women were a big part of rodeo then and were involved in many ways. At early rodeos, women competed head-to-head with the men. Then, as big shows gained popularity, women were spotlighted. Lady bronc riders actually became paid contract acts, with five or six women riding, including Alice and Margie Greenough, Tad Lucas, and Lucille Mulhall. The producers even carried a special "girls' string" of broncs that were smaller than the men's broncs and "showy," or wild looking.

It is speculated that in the early part of the century, women on ranches were left home to break the colts while the men were doing other jobs—thus making the women proficient bronc riders. As roles for women in society changed, fewer women tried their hand at riding rough stock in competition.

Women who didn't care for bronc riding could get into the rodeo act as Sponsor Girls or Ranch Girls—beautiful cowgirls hired as public relations representatives. They did radio interviews and carried flags in the grand entry ceremony.

Trick riding was also an option as a paid act which featured brave and talented women. Jerry Ann Portwood Taylor was one of those beauties, and reminisced, "I was only 15 years old when I went to New York, and we all saw things we'd never seen . . . I never wanted to go back to the country! Most of the Ranch Girls became barrel racers, but I had seen Fay Blesing trick riding—she was so glamorous—and I liked the glamour and clothes—so I decided to become a trick rider."

In the early 1930s, cars became a more common mode of transportation to rodeos, and the big shows continued to entertain large crowds. The popularity of the rodeo is clear as Mitzi Riley recalls that the Madison Square Garden Rodeo in 1944 ran for fifty-four performances over six weeks.

These rodeo heydays, however, were short-lived. Maybe it was the depression and their need for steady pay, but women's involvement in rodeo gradually diminished. By the 1940s, lady bronc riders as paid performers were a thing of the past, and Ranch Girls faded away after the late 1940s.

Instead, women competed in cutting events and began creating their own contests, like barrel racing. It has been said that barrel racing began as a friendly challenge of horsemanship skills, with the barrels set up in a straight line and the contestants weaving in a "slalom" pattern. Eventually the cloverleaf pattern was established. In 1948, the Girls Rodeo Association (GRA) was formed to standardize rules, judging, and record keeping in this and other events. The Rodeo Cowboys Association (RCA, now PRCA) and the GRA have operated separately since then.

That first year, there were seventy-four charter members of the GRA, led by Margaret Owens, and sixty approved events with a total payoff of $29,000. Records indicate that championships were awarded in cutting horse, calf roping, ribbon roping, team tying, bull riding, barrel racing, and bareback riding. In 1951, there was also a saddle bronc riding champion acknowledged. Throughout the years, as new events became popular, they were added to the GRA competition. Flag racing, team tying, ribbon roping, steer undecorating, pole bending, and goat tying, are all events that have come and gone over the past four decades.

14

In 1982, The GRA was renamed as The Women's Professional Rodeo Association, and since then the WPRA has expanded its goals to include larger purses, bigger and better rodeos, and greater public recognition of women's rodeo. The WPRA now boasts 1,600 members and a payoff of nearly $2 million.

Today, 125 of the 1,600 WPRA members compete in the All Women's events—bareback and bull riding, calf roping (both breakaway and tie-down) and team roping. Ironically, while women's rodeo has evolved in many areas, the number of entrants in the rough stock events has neither grown nor declined; there are still only a dozen or so of these brave ladies!

The world of rodeo and the women involved in the sport have seen a lot of change through the years. Pioneer rodeo women like Vera McGinnis Farra and Mabel DeLong Strickland would have never imagined that in the year 1993 a barrel racing champion, Charmayne James-Rodman, would win over $18,000 at the Houston Livestock Show and collect more than $1 million in her ten years as a WPRA member. And that sponsor girls would be replaced by rodeo queens and Miss Rodeo America, who continue to preserve the grace, beauty, and tradition of the rodeo.

So, the rodeo winnings have changed, among other things, but a few aspects of the rodeo remain the same—like the cowgirls' integrity, grit and determination. The history of many brave cowgirls from all walks of life are documented at the National Cowgirl Hall of Fame and Western Heritage Center. Many have been inducted and honored for their contribution to the sport of rodeo and for meeting the challenge of the West. But all cowgirls, whether recognized for their part in rodeo history or quietly tending to the needs of ranch and family, are the stuff of which legends are made.

Pam Minick and Jimmie Gibbs-Munroe

PAM MINICK, a former Miss Rodeo America and 1982 Women's World Champion Calf Roper, has been the Vice President and Publicity Director of the WPRA since 1978. The recipient of many awards, she was named the 1992 Coca-Cola Woman of the Year in Pro Rodeo. Her talents have also led her to appear in several movies and commercials, in addition to frequent appearances as sports commentator and host on television.

JIMMIE GIBBS-MUNROE is a former intercollegiate rodeo champion and 1975 GRA (WPRA) World Champion Barrel Racer. Having joined the WPRA in 1974, Jimmie has devoted her time as president of the organization since 1978. For her contributions to the sport of rodeo, she received the Coca-Cola Woman of the Year award in 1990 and was inducted into the National Cowgirl Hall of Fame in 1992.

REINE HAFLEY SHELTON
1902–1979

Born into show business, Reine Hafley made her vaudeville debut at three years old as part of her mother Mamie Francis's sharpshooting act. A year later Reine and her mother were touring with Pawnee Bill's Wild West Show. A riding professional at only four years old, she was reared in the camps of this century's most famous western exhibitions.

In 1909, Mamie Francis married Wild West show promoter and entrepreneur California Frank Hafley. Seven-year-old Reine served both as trick and bronc rider, and as an oriental or flamenco dancer. An eager performer, she also rode elephants in those early shows.

At sixteen, while still touring with Wild West shows, Reine made her competitive debut and quickly achieved fame on the rodeo circuit. In her first year she gathered a second-place trick riding finish at Cheyenne Frontier Days and a third in the event at Fort Worth's annual Fat Stock Show and Rodeo. Two years later she rode in the first Madison Square Garden Rodeo and returned in 1924 to claim the bronc riding title.

That same year, Reine, by now an established star, met future world-champion cowboy Dick Shelton. They married in June of the following year and together pursued rodeo careers.

Famous for her beauty and daring, Reine's trademark stunt routinely terrified audiences as she pretended to fall from her horse's hips. Expecting to witness her death, crowds cheered as she pulled her feet together and held herself in a perfect tail stand. An exceptional talent, she had taught western legend Tad Lucas to trick ride while they both toured with a traveling Wild West show early in their careers.

Equally talented on the racetrack, Reine jockeyed in popular pony express-style relays, in which riders quickly changed horses, moved tack, and vaulted into the saddle at full speed. Champions had to win a series of relays, often staged at every performance of multi-day rodeos. In 1927, while racing in San Antonio, she won all but one of the relays. Her horse fell at a turn, yet she remounted and still finished second in the difficult race.

At the height of their fame, Dick and Reine Shelton retired to a Texas ranch in 1938. Though no longer in competition, Reine couldn't stay away from rodeo and often worked as a pickup rider, helping other rough-stock contestants safely dismount from a completed ride.

Ruth Parton Webster
1895–1978

Hailed as the World's Champion Woman Relay Racer, tiny Ruth Parton delighted crowds and defeated champions in her long career.

Ruth lived on the Yakima Indian Reservation at Toppenish, Washington. Encouraged by her parents, she began racing swift thoroughbreds at thirteen. Success on the track led to rodeo appearances and the then-popular, rough sport of relay racing.

Relays, inspired by the country's fascination with the short-lived pony express, required jockeys to race at full speed, stop instantly, switch their saddle to a waiting horse, vault on its back, and dash to the next relay station. The demanding routine was repeated until reaching the finish line. Racing was the most popular event at western rodeos, and champions won the acclaim of the crowd and exceptional prize money. One-thousand-dollar purses were not uncommon in women's competition.

At sixteen, Ruth Parton entered her first relay. Set to ride against the winning Irwin sisters, Ruth was barred from the track by Wild West show patriarch Charlie Irwin—perhaps to protect Ruth, or more likely his daughters' careers. The reasons for his action are still hazy, but Ruth vowed to ride against the girls and "make them and their haughty father eat some of their dust."

With six of the fastest and best-bred Canadian fillies, and tutored by renowned pony express rider Sleepy Armstrong, Ruth began to win ladies' races and in 1916 defeated the Irwin girls and a field of talented riders to claim Cheyenne's first prize. She repeated her success in 1917 to become one of the few cowgirls ever to win the Frontier Days' coveted *Denver Post* trophy for best female rider in two consecutive years.

The Parton Ranch trained champion thoroughbreds while Ruth jockeyed at Canada's and Mexico's popular tracks. She retired from racing in 1929. For her contributions to the sport, her fellow native Washingtonians call Ruth Parton the "Mother of Thoroughbred Racing."

As described by her noted biographer, Reba Perry Blakely, "Ruth, at seventy-three, was still training her own race horses, ponying them, caring for them, and drilling two-year-olds with the same grace and charm that made her one of the most beloved women in the whole horse world—a lovely, tiny, dimple-cheeked woman with grey hair and soft grace now, but with strong traces of the startling beauty that made her an outstanding personality of early-day rodeo."

OLLIE OSBORN
1896–1989

Listening to the crowd applaud the famous relay-riding Irwin sisters, twelve-year-old Ollie Osborn knew what she wanted to do, and four years later she was ready.

Though she was given no hope of even placing at the local Union Livestock Shows, Ollie rode full speed and deftly switched her saddle in the relay event to claim her first victory. Encouraged by the win, she was determined to compete at the Pendleton Roundup, where she captured an overall second place. The daughter of Grande Ronde Valley, Oregon, homestead ranchers was on her way to a professional rodeo career.

Relays were by far the most popular event at the western rodeos Ollie frequented, but, following her early racing success, Ollie tried a different event. In Walla Walla, Washington, while traveling the competitive Northwest racing circuit, Ollie rode her first bucking bronc and earned twenty-five dollars for the exhibition.

In 1916, Ollie, along with her brother George, joined C. B. Irwin's traveling rodeo. Crossing the country by private train, the Wild West troupe moved from Cheyenne on to Kansas City, Omaha, and Canton and spent eleven days entertaining in New York City. Ollie returned in time to compete at the Pendleton Roundup, where the world championship title again eluded the young rider.

Though women riders of her day often fastened their stirrups together with a rawhide hobble, Ollie is perhaps best remembered for riding "slick" at Pendleton's premier event. "Hobbles made for an easy ride," she said. "You could point your toes out, heels in, and keep a good, deep seat in the saddle. But I rode like the men, and it made for some wild rides."

Remembered for her daring rides and fabulous tailor-made clothes, Ollie's most prized possession was a wardrobe trunk of costumes and memorabilia from her rodeo career. It contained, among other memories, a photo album she called "butterflies for her golden years."

Ollie continued to ride professionally until 1932. Among the honors in her successful career, she claimed the most relay victories at the livestock show in her hometown of Union, Oregon. "We can't say it isn't dangerous," Ollie Osborn once said. "We know better, it is dangerous. But . . . when you're young, and everybody's feeling good, and the band's playing, it just gives you a go-ahead."

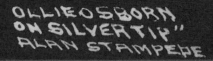
OLLIE OSBORN
ON SILVERTIP"
ALAN STAMPEDE

RUTH SCANTLIN ROACH SALMON
1896–1986

Truly charmed by the promise of show business, in 1912 Ruth Roach ran away from her Missouri home. She returned a year later, not destitute and asking forgiveness, but riding proudly through the streets of Kansas City, Missouri, in the 101 Ranch Wild West Show parade.

Ruth and her husband Bryan performed with the respected troupe, where she learned the finer points of trick riding from her friends and fellow performers Lucille Mulhall and Prairie Rose Henderson. While performing in London, England, the 101's popular 1914 engagement was ended by the advent of World War I. The English government seized the show's vehicles, stable gear, and livestock—including Ruth Roach's beloved horses—for its army.

Ruth's competitive debut came at America's first indoor rodeo, the 1917 Fort Worth Roundup, produced by Lucille Mulhall in conjunction with the annual Fat Stock Show. Needing a cowgirl bronc rider, Mulhall asked Ruth to tackle a wild horse known as Memphis Blue. Ruth watched one of the cowboys ride, quickly agreed, and claimed the $100 first-place prize. She was the first woman to ride a bronc at the Fort Worth contest, and the event remained a favorite.

Sporting her trademark giant hair bows and boots hand-tooled with hearts, Ruth continued to compete and in 1919 captured first-place finishes in both the Fort Worth and Cheyenne bronc riding contests. Dubbed the "soft-spoken, rough-riding golden girl of the West," she was named champion lady bronc rider of Chicago's 1920 Roundup.

In 1923, as part of a Wild West show, Ruth performed before President Warren Harding in the nation's capital and the following year returned to London with a group of top contestants as part of Tex Austin's traveling rodeo. As many as 92,000 fans attended the first performance in Wembly Stadium.

After winning 1932's Madison Square Garden bronc riding competition, her last great prize, Ruth continued to compete until she married rancher Fred Salmon in 1938 and moved to his home in Nocona, Texas.

Once hired for a publicity stunt, the sparkling performer is remembered for trick riding up the steps, across the lobby, and through the dining room of Fort Worth's Texas Hotel.

A pioneer woman bronc rider with flying blonde curls and exuberant style, Ruth Roach earned the admiration of rodeo fans. "Of all the features at the Fat Stock Show and Rodeo," a 1919 *Star Telegram* photo caption read, "none is more thrilling than the riding of Ruth Roach, cowgirl."

MABEL DELONG STRICKLAND
1897–1976

I know you think I'm a paradox," said rodeo legend Mabel Strickland in an interview during her winning career, "but I belong in the saddle for I've been there since I was three . . . Still, I love dresses and everything that goes with them."

At the start of her career, Mabel, already a winning relay racer, won Walla Walla's trick riding in 1913, 1914, and 1915. A renowned beauty, she was an established celebrity when she married respected cowboy Hugh Strickland and with his assistance added steer roping to her accomplishments. At the Dewey Roundup, her first roping, she posted a record time of 21.2 seconds, unbeaten for two years. She often bested leading cowboy ropers.

Though the young couple tried to settle down and farm near Mountain Home, Idaho, mounting debts and ever-increasing prize money lured them back to the rodeo. As winner of the prestigious McAlpin trophy in 1922, presented to Cheyenne's all-around cowgirl, Mabel was a natural favorite for success at the first Madison Square Garden Rodeo later that year. Mabel tied Bonnie Gray for the trick riding, and in 1923 both returned for New York's two major rodeos where Mabel dominated, collecting more than $2,000 in combined prize money.

Mabel first competed on broncs when arena director Eddie McCarty, who needed an extra woman rider, entered her name. "You can ride as well as any of them," he said. She finished second.

In 1924, a group of cowgirls, including Mabel—a winner that year of her third Madison Square Garden title—petitioned the Pendleton Roundup Association to compete equally with cowboys. They hoped to garner the all-around title, an unprecedented challenge in rodeo history. Permission was denied. Despite the controversial dispute, in 1927 Mabel reigned as first rodeo queen and set a steer roping record at the Northwest contest.

Performing with Bing Crosby in the 1936 *Rhythm on the Range*, Mabel enjoyed Hollywood success and founded the Association of Film Equestriennes, a group of hard-riding rodeo actresses.

Changes occurred for Mabel in 1941. Women saw the end of their major rodeo contests, Hugh Strickland died, and Mabel retired. She later remarried and raised champion Appaloosa horses.

As remembered by rodeo personality Fog Horn Clancy, "It was worth the price of admission to a rodeo just to see her ride across the arena. There was never a girl who sat a horse more perfectly . . ."

Lable Strickland
Queen
Of The Pendleton
Round Up
1927

VERA MCGINNIS FARRA
1895–1990

At a Salt Lake City rodeo in 1913, Vera McGinnis discovered the girls' relay race needed another rider. She volunteered without letting on she'd never even seen the event. Arriving at the track in time to observe one of the riders make her run, the novice simply followed suit.

The next day, Vera quit her secretarial job for relay racing, but on the third day, her horse failed to slow as it approached the switch-over to her final mount. She remembered coming to on her fourth horse as she neared the finish line with her first-place position being overtaken by two other riders. Vera finished last with a headache, one tooth missing, and two teeth bent, but the producer was so impressed that he signed her up to go to Canada.

In 1917, Vera worked with movies as a horse wrangler, movie extra, and stuntwoman but was soon back to rodeoing. "I don't care what I do as long as I can do it on horseback."

In 1921, Vera was in Hawaii, giving exhibitions in bronc, bull, and trick riding. Then in 1924, she sailed to London with Tex Austin's troupe for a sixteen-day, thirty-two-performance stand, winning the trick riding and ladies' relay racing. After the highly acclaimed production, Vera and seven others stayed on for a month-long showing at the Coliseum, with Vera racing across the stage, doing her famous under-the-belly crawl. They took in Ireland, where Vera won a cup at Dublin's first rodeo, and went to France and Belgium before returning to the States.

Vera joined a troupe touring the Orient in 1925. The days were so hot in Singapore that performances were scheduled for 9:15 in the evening. The troupe reached country towns by dilapidated riverboat. Food was scarce and poor, and the contestants packed along the leaky tents they used for shelter. Two-hour performances were somehow managed with five saddle horses and eight people. Pay was slow and sometimes nonexistent. For the trip home, Vera could only manage passage for herself and was forced to leave her horse behind.

Before more than 20,000 spectators at Livermore, California, Vera's daring career came to a violent end in 1934, when her horse fell and rolled, puncturing Vera's lung and breaking her hip, neck, back, and most of her ribs. She was told she wouldn't likely live and definitely would never walk, but she defied the odds by walking out of the hospital five weeks later, using only a cane.

MILDRED DOUGLAS CHRISMAN
1895–1983

A genuine love of animals and an early fascination with the circus convinced Mildred Douglas that her destiny lie in the exciting world of animals and show business. Rodeo was a natural choice.

Mildred's father, a professor of mechanical engineering at the University of Pennsylvania, sent her to an exclusive Connecticut boarding school, where she soon discovered her love of horses. It wasn't long before she left home and found a job riding stock at the famous Miller Brothers 101 Ranch.

She not only rode her first bucking horse at the Royal Stock Show in Kansas City, Missouri, but Mildred also, for the first time, attempted trick riding on Lucille Mulhall's horse with some last-minute coaching by the Wild West show legend. The following year brought Cheyenne and Pendleton bronc riding titles. Philadelphia native Mildred Douglas was acclaimed as "The World's Champion Girl Bronc Rider."

With husband Tommie Douglas, Mildred traveled with the circus, performing a variety of acts including trick rider, trick shooter, and animal trainer. Of her performances she said, "In addition to performing with trained horses, I also worked with a lion act, fooled around with elephants, and had a leopard for a pet."

A friendship with Tom Mix from their 101 Ranch days brought the Douglases to Hollywood. Mildred had parts in several of the cowboy star's films and met Pat Chrisman, original owner and trainer of the star's celebrated movie horse, Tony. Twelve years later, the pair renewed their acquaintance and married in 1933.

During their lives together, Mildred and Pat toured the country with "Aristocratic Goats," an act of performing Angoras, with one that walked a tightrope. Pat later trained a dog for Mildred to use while entertaining soldiers during World War II. The couple settled in Lawton, Oklahoma, where together they trained animals for a variety of Vaudeville-style acts. Pat Chrisman died in 1953.

Far from finished with her career, at age fifty-nine Mildred Douglas Chrisman returned to school to fulfill one of her childhood dreams, becoming a nurse. She practiced for more than twenty years and at age seventy-nine joined the staff of a Lawton doctor.

MILDRED DOUGLAS RIDING WILD STEER.

Barbara Inez "Tad" Lucas
1902–1990

Tad Lucas, the youngest of twenty-four children, had her first professional experience at the fair in Gordon, Nebraska, where neighbors enlisted the teenager as a jockey. While there she competed against Mildred Douglas and won a twenty-five-dollar prize for steer riding. "Well," Tad said, "that ruined me, right there."

Though she rode steers, broncs, and popular relays, Lucas earned her rodeo fame as a daring and inventive trick rider. Tutored by Reine Hafley, Tad made her trick riding debut in 1924 at Tex Austin's rodeo in London, England, and in her career collected all of the major trophies and titles available to rodeo cowgirls. Tad's outstanding trick riding coupled with her strong rough stock events and relays often combined to capture the all-around title.

From 1928–1930 Tad won Madison Square Garden's prestigious MGM trophy established by the movie studio as a "tribute to the charm and courage of western womanhood" and, as a three-year winner, retired the prize. Lucas donated the $10,000 trophy to the National Cowboy Hall of Fame in Oklahoma City, where it is currently displayed.

Tad's career nearly ended in 1933. While competing in trick riding, she was caught by her horse's hooves and permanently lost the use of her left arm, which remained in a cast for three years. Joined by her five-year-old daughter Mitzi, then making her performance debut, Lucas returned to contract trick riding a scant year later.

"There were a lot of tricks I could do with one hand," she said. "But, I had learned all that when I had two arms." Renowned for her inventive style, Lucas created the back drag, hanging her head dangerously near the horse's running hooves with her feet secured in straps behind the saddle.

In 1940, Tad won her first bronc riding title at Cheyenne Frontier Days and brought home a Sidney, Australia, first-place finish.

Tad continued to perform and give exhibition trick rides until her retirement at age fifty-six. "The rodeos weren't using trick riders so much anymore," she explained. "A trick rider would starve to death if that's all he did . . . I figured it would be a good time to quit."

Tad's stunning versatility allowed her to compete on both the western circuit, where relay races captured the audience's esteem, and the eastern circuit, where broncs and trick riding were a cowgirl's main events.

Described in an early newspaper account as "the world's greatest female rider," Tad Lucas, a true queen of the arena, died in 1990.

GOLDIA BAYS "FIELDS" MALONE
1903–

Goldia Fields's rodeo career began with a challenge when the Triangle Ranch Rodeo offered $10 to anyone who could ride an outlaw horse. Sixteen-year-old Goldia volunteered. Thrown the first time, she refused to quit and claimed her prize.

A few months later Goldia was thrilled by a Wild West show featuring trick rider Curly Griffith. "That's for me," she decided. "That's what I'm going to do."

After a transfer in 1920 from her railroad restaurant job in Childress, Texas, Goldia moved to Fort Worth, where she arranged to exercise Griffith's horses to pay for trick riding lessons. She quickly mastered several stunts and began to perform locally under the stage name Goldia Fields. "I was world famous before my mother ever found out what I was doing," Fields explains. "For years and years I rode under the name Goldia Fields so she wouldn't know . . . ."

At the 1922 Fort Worth Fat Stock Show and Rodeo, where Goldia fell with a horse she was exercising, the cowgirl in training met Bob Malone, who immediately hired her as a bronc and trick rider for his previously all-male troupe. Her contract provided room, board, and expenses, but her salary depended on gate receipts.

After Bob and Goldia's Valentines Day wedding in 1926, the happy couple moved to a Texas farm. "I worked for him for four years," Goldia remembers. Her husband joked that he married her so that she would work for nothing.

As part of Malone's show, Goldia could not be contented with the broncs reserved for women riders. "For two years," she remembers, "I rode every bronc they brought in." Goldia was the only woman ever to ride Texas Bud Snell's famous outlaw, Funeral Wagon.

Goldia's last performance was at the Double Heart Ranch of Sweetwater, Texas, on August 18, 1932. While herding cattle later that year, Goldia's horse collided with a cow, and she was crushed beneath her mount. The horse was unharmed, the cow sustained a few broken ribs, but Goldia suffered extensive internal injuries, requiring three-and-a-half hours of delicate surgery. The freak accident ended her career.

Turning her attention to the family farm, Goldia managed the property alone after Bob's death and was several times honored for her exceptional service to youth organizations. The woman who rode horses as a teenager to the town watering hole for extra money was the first woman honorary member of the Future Farmers of America (FFA).

BONNIE JEAN GRAY HARRIS
1891–1988

Bonnie Gray's riding aspirations began when in 1897 her parents gave her a gift—her first horse. Bonnie was six years old.

Competing at major shows across the country, rodeo's "King Tut Cowgirl" tied with Mabel Strickland for the trick riding championship at the first successful New York City rodeo, the 1922 Madison Square Garden event. A coin toss gave Strickland the trophy, but Gray, concentrating more heavily on the western arena circuit, continued to amaze crowds with her daring stunts and inventive tricks.

Following her success at her first New York City Rodeo, Bonnie and the enthusiastic crowds returned in 1923 for two major shows, another at Madison Square Garden and one at Yankee Stadium. Bonnie and her trick-riding rival Mabel Strickland were the only women to perform in both events.

The cowgirls of Bonnie's day were darlings of the media, welcoming the curiosity and adoration of the American public. Perhaps nowhere were the women more toasted than in the early years of New York City's legendary contest. The lady rough rider socialized with celebrities, such as General Pershing, tenor Enrico Caruso, and England's Prince of Wales (later titled Duke of Windsor). A *Billboard* account at the time of that first Madison Square Garden Rodeo announced that New York was "rodeo mad."

With her horse at full gallop, Bonnie was one of the first cowgirls to ride under the horse's belly and, surprisingly, was never injured performing this hazardous stunt. In later years similar moves became the standard of fancy trick riding.

At her wedding to Donald Harris, where all the participants—even the minister—were horseback, the Washington-state native celebrated by jumping her massive Palomino, King Tut, over a touring car with her new husband and maid of honor sitting bravely inside. Bonnie had performed this same stunt to the delight of audiences at major rodeos from Cheyenne to Pendleton.

A true pioneer of women's rodeo, Bonnie Gray is believed to have been the first woman in the world to ride bulls at Mexico's bullfights. In addition to delighting audiences with her daring riding, as Hollywood's western film industry grew, she became a pioneer woman in a new arena, as stunt rider and double for the greatest stars of her day. Hoot Gibson, himself an accomplished rider, Tim McCoy, Helen Twelvetrees, Tom Mix, and Ken Maynard all benefited from Bonnie's talents. "I knew all the big stars," she remembers, "from Mary Pickford on down."

LUCYLE GARNER RICHARDS
1909–

In 1909, Lucyle Garner was born to a Choctaw/Dutch mother and Cherokee/second-generation Irish-immigrant father. Her early memories include excursions on the Oklahoma reservation ranch, perched behind her father's saddle.

At age twelve, Lucyle was abandoned by her parents to an empty house with only a cardboard suitcase containing her meager possessions. The nearest neighbor reported seeing her parents ride past, "spitting blood." Lucyle climbed on her scrawny pony and rode to the Indian boarding school she attended, where she gained work as a dishwasher. She would never see her mother again.

At a Talihena rodeo a year later, Lucyle caught the attention of the producer, who queried local cowboys about her riding abilities. "Sure, she rides horses, if you have anything that'll buck!" they told him.

Lucyle remembered, "My hair was so long it hit the horse on the head as he bucked forward, then on the tail as he rocked backward," but she stayed astride long enough to get hooked. "When they bucked me off, I'd almost cry until I could get back on again."

More than ready to be free of the constraints of school, Lucyle changed her name to prevent her father from finding her when she ran away to be with Cherokee Hammond's Wild West Show. "I told the rodeo boss I wanted a job riding broncs . . . he asked my age. I stretched the truth a bit and tried to stand taller than I was, giving my age as eighteen. He looked at me—you could tell he was just dying to bust out laughing, then he said, 'Okay.' "

Lucyle's first tour lasted four months, until homesickness won out, but launched a half-century career of bulldogging, rough riding, calf roping, trick roping, and trick riding. She called trick riding "sissy stuff," part of her rodeo contracts she hated but performed with precision and flair.

Lucyle joined the international circuit and tried her hand at riding Mexico's sleek, monstrous, black fighting bulls. "I promised myself that if ever I got out of Mexico alive from riding those fighting bulls, I'd never go there again!"

Lucyle Garner Richards strived for excellence in every area of interest, but one that captivated her fully was the desire to become a world-renowned "cowgirl Amelia Earhart." She entered long-distance races and compiled a repertoire of over a dozen hazardous aerobatic stunts. "It's just like trick riding. All you have to do is keep your head and dash into it . . . careless-like."

Isora DeRacy Young
1905–

Isora DeRacy Young moved to Pecos, Texas, in 1924, where she worked as a deputy sheriff. She joined a roping club, practicing several times a week with the local cowboys, and entered regional roping events. Isora says she would "rope anything or anytime, anywhere they'd let me."

Her first big show was the Double Heart Ranch Rodeo in Sweetwater, Texas, where she won the saddle in the sponsor contest, often pole bending, barrel or flag racing. At Van Horn, Texas, Isora competed in both sponsor and roping events. "Then someone there called Colonel Johnson, and he called and told me that he'd like for me to go to Madison Square Garden. I was thrilled to death, but I couldn't go . . . The sheriff would not give me leave to go and keep my job."

However, Isora contested in the Colonel's show at Sidney, Iowa. "We had to rope for a set fee per calf if we tied it—nothing if we missed. You miss few under those circumstances! In fact, one had to be calf-roping mad to be on the road in the first place."

At a rodeo in Salinas, California, Abe Lefton announced, "Here is the gal from Texas who can rope and tie a 300-pound calf in less time than I can wrap a pound of hamburger."

Isora remembers, "I felt ten feet tall!"

Touring with Milt Hinkle, Isora was sent to buy a calf for roping. "I roped that same calf twice a day all season. When it was ended, the calf must have weighed 400 pounds, but he had been caught and tied so many times that all I had to do was catch him, grab his leg; he would fall over and let me tie him in record time, for he hardly moved [a] muscle."

Car trouble plagued Isora's trip to Reno, Nevada. She arrived out of money and reluctant to send home for more. Instructed where to leave her horse, she felt relieved it would be cared for so well.

A surprise greeted her when the show ended. "When I got ready to leave, I was presented with a bill for my horse, and it was staggering! . . . I told 'em I couldn't pay it right then . . . What could I do? And he said, 'Well, you can get a shovel and clean out the horse stalls.'

"I stayed there two days and cleaned stalls, but I did a good job! . . . Such things make life interesting."

LORRAINE GRAHAM ROQUEPLOT SHOUTZ
1920–

Lorraine Graham surely has been an inspiration to legions of American girls with rodeo and horseback dreams. Known to her audiences as "Baby Lorraine," she began her riding career at age four, performing popular tricks and daring stunts, perched bravely on the back of surefooted, fleet ponies.

The star attraction in the Graham Company of eight riding brothers and sisters, Lorraine with strength, ability, and skill far beyond her years, set many national records in trick and fancy riding, roping, and perhaps most astonishing, the physically demanding contest of bulldogging. The family group was the brainchild of Lorraine's father, Oley, who trained each of the accomplished young riders. Having fallen on hard times in the rodeo arena around 1927 when jobs were few, Oley Graham set about creating a highly sought-after entertainment group, planning to make his children the greatest team of trick riders in America.

Often performing with governors, senators, or congressmen in the stands, Baby Lorraine raced around the arena deftly standing on her head in the saddle, slipping back on her horse's haunches, and entertaining thousands of appreciative fans. She quickly and expertly, with skill equal to any of the circuit's acclaimed tricksters, rode through a series of horseback acrobatics, heart-stopping to even the most seasoned riders, frightening and irresistible to the audience.

Fearless riding, eager performances, and near-flawless execution won the young daredevil the hearts of the fans and top honors at the Calgary Stampede, Pendleton Roundup, Denver's National Western Stock Show, Cheyenne Frontier Days, and Madison Square Garden, among other shows. Each of the eight children was an outstanding rider, but it was Lorraine Graham, along with her brother Ralph, who received the group's top billing. The unique Graham Company performances were top attractions at the Kansas City Royal and the Chicago International Livestock shows. An appealing mixture of agility, strength, and youthful exuberance, in the 1930s Baby Lorraine was crowned the World's Champion Juvenile Trick Rider.

With the company's success and the enthusiastic public reaction to its star performer Baby Lorraine, Oley Graham became the father of the most popular act of its kind. Perennial rodeo favorites, Graham's children performed stunts as they rode into fame and the colorful history of the trick riding event.

For her excellence in the sport and stunning horsemanship, Lorraine Graham Roqueplot Shoultz was honored with a 1981 induction into the National Cowgirl Hall of Fame.

GENE KRIEG CREED
1909–1993

Young Gene Krieg loved startling townspeople with her daring, full-speed charge down the main street of her hometown, Holly, Colorado, standing atop a galloping steed. In local circles, she became known for her skill in riding wild calves. A private longing to challenge rodeo's rough stock burned in her heart.

At sixteen, she was discharged by rail to her sister's to assist after the birth of a nephew. However, a *Denver Post* article publicizing the 1925 Cheyenne Frontier Days convinced Gene to switch trains and follow her dream of sun-tailing broncs.

She entered the ladies' bronc riding with a borrowed saddle and jockey suit. The third and last ride of the five-day event found Gene mistakenly turned loose on one of the rankest horses intended for the men's competition. Gene rode "slick" like the men, with unhobbled stirrups, and was proclaimed the "new queen of hearts and hard horses."

With her prizes of a silver trophy buckle, a $75 Stetson, and $300, she resolutely headed down rodeo road for the next program of events. She was sporting one of two new custom-tailored costumes when she cashed in more winnings in Monte Vista, Colorado.

Rodeo producers Verne Elliott and Eddie McCarty persuaded Gene to pitch in with their outfit. Hardly hesitating, she took up their challenge of hazardous trick riding and relay racing with typical fearlessness and natural balance. The youthful cowgirl soon won hearts with her dimpled smile, pleasant manner, and deceptively frail appearance.

Gene's career spanned the continent from the Pendleton Round-Up in Oregon to New York's Madison Square Garden. International laurels followed a royal command performance in London, England, and the Easter Royal Agricultural Show in Sidney, Australia. "Down under," Gene was given six weeks to break and train a wild horse ready for the performances.

Her star-spangled career took a tragic turn in 1941 before a stunned Madison Square Garden crowd. Like a delicate reed stretched above her elegant white mount, Gene stood atop Sheik for a wild gallop around the perimeters of the arena and prepared to fall backwards into the "suicide drag." Thoughtlessly, a spectator tossed her white mink coat across the rail ahead of the speeding pair and startled Sheik into an abrupt stop that threw Gene to the wrong side, where she dangled helplessly. An intended rescuer spooked Sheik further, and the horse swung around, slamming Gene's head against the concrete wall. The freak injury robbed Gene of her natural balance and prematurely ended her bold, spirited career.

ALICE ANDERSON ADAMS HOLDEN
1907–1994

An advertisement for pretty girls to ride in a parade forever changed the life of bronc riding star Alice Adams. Together with two cousins, Alice took the riding job, but, unlike her companions, she never returned to the life she once knew. In 1925, Alice Adams joined the rodeo.

"Many a jackpot was made up just to see me tackle an 'impossible' bronc," Alice remembered. She earned her reputation as one of the finest women bronc riders in the business. "I rode steers, broncs, trick rode, drove chuck wagon, and raced chariots with four unbroken wild broncos right off the plains, hitched and eared down for the starting signal," she said, showing the pluck that made her a highly sought-after participant for the best rodeos of her time.

Abandoning demonstration riding for the more lucrative competitive arena, Alice, who had been riding since the age of five, twice won the world championship bronc riding title at Madison Square Garden and in 1928 collected two international titles in Cuba.

"I did a couple of seasons in the circus, made a movie, played, danced all night, and had a wonderful time," Alice reflected.

Like so many of her early women's rodeo counterparts, Alice attracted the attention of Hollywood's entertainment community and got her chance at movie stardom in a silent film called *Jack the Whipper*. As her fame grew, so did her legend. Flamboyant publicity man and early rodeo talent manager Fog Horn Clancy wrote factual accounts of her career and, according to Alice, fictionalized her life in in his highly popular western-romance-magazine stories.

After retiring from the arena, Alice remained active in the rodeo world, working as a booking agent, writing advertising, making personal appearances, or serving as time and payroll clerk for rodeos across the country. The Iowa native was arena secretary for Fay Kirkwood's first all cowgirl rodeo, her participation in the sport spanning two unique eras of rodeo competition.

Truly a life guided by chance, Alice met her second husband, Guy Holden, at a Nowato, Oklahoma, rodeo as he ran from the stands to assist her when her horse collided with another rider's mount. The couple moved to Guy's Craig County ranch. World-champion rider Alice Adams Holden traded her rodeo riggings for a ranch saddle.

Looking back on a life filled with rodeo prize money, media attention, and pitching broncs, Alice says simply, "It was so easy."

VAUGHN KRIEG HUSKEY
1904–1976

In 1926, Vaughn Krieg covered remaining trick riding contracts for her sister Gene, who had suffered a ruptured appendix, and never went back to her family farm. Leaving behind her ex-husband and one young son, Vaughn took her six-month-old son on the circuit and within a year became one of the leading bronc riders.

Born on a Colorado ranch, Vaughn soon added bull-dogging to her skills and at a Roswell, New Mexico, contest wrestled a steer to the ground despite the pain of a broken shoulder. Hired for a promotion at a Kansas event, Vaughn became the first woman to bulldog a steer from the running board of a moving automobile. She helped introduce the DeSoto automobile to American consumers. A popular contract performer, Vaughn was also successful in rodeo competition and in 1937 captured her greatest win, the Madison Square Garden bronc riding title. She soon settled on an Oklahoma ranch with her new husband, rodeo cowboy Lynn Huskey. The couple built a private rodeo arena and clubhouse to display their many trophies. In 1937, they began to produce contests entered by many of their colleagues from the professional rodeo circuit.

In a crowd-pleasing act, Vaughn, dressed as an elderly audience member, would sit in the stands and wait for the announcer to declare a bronc too rank for any cowgirl or cowboy to dare ride. Leaping to her feet, Vaughn would yell, "I'll ride that bronc." Then to the crowd's delight, she would dash into the arena, climb into the chute and show her championship bucking style.

At these 1930s events, Vaughn Huskey became one of the few women producers in rodeo history. As a producer and as a bulldogger she made great contributions to the sport.

In 1942, Vaughn formed the Flying V All Cowgirl Rodeo company, planning to provide entertainment for military bases. Her lone event at the Lamar County Fairgrounds near Paris, Texas, was one of the first ever all-female rodeos. Vaughn directed a competitive program of six professional events, one sponsor contest, and three contract acts. In addition to management responsibilities, she competed in bronc riding, bulldogging, steer riding, and calf roping. It was the only all-girl event Vaughn produced. World War II made travel increasingly difficult, and rodeo, like many American spectator sports, suffered lean years before victory.

As described by her son, John McKinney, Vaughn Krieg "was a lady of courage and guts . . . a forerunner of today's liberated woman."

MARY WILLIAMS PARKS
1910–

Mary Williams was born and raised on her family's Colorado ranch. "I rode after and took care of cattle from the time I was big enough to stay in the saddle. My mother and I broke most all of our horses . . . After my brothers and I was older we started making the rodeos close to home. I rode steers and bare back horses at first, then started riding saddle broncs." Her father's disapproval of Mary's rodeoing didn't stop her at age seventeen from riding her horse over 250 miles alone to compete in Cheyenne, Wyoming. It was the determined beginning of a career that would take off three years later.

A 1935 New York paper described Mary: "Barely over five feet tall, she's the smallest bronk riding cowgirl in the world. A mere slip of a girl, bashful and pretty, with a dazzling shock of light curly hair, she rides her leaping and prancing bronk with skill and daring, reflecting the true atmosphere of the old West."

With husband Bill, Mary crisscrossed the continent and competed internationally. "In 1936, we drove our car to Prince Albert, Saskatchewan, in Canada. We put the car in storage and boarded a rodeo train. Margie Greenough and I were the two lady bronc riders contracted for the tour . . . Married couples had compartments at one end of the train, while the single cowboys bunked in other Pullman cars. We had our own cook and lived in close family style . . .

"We could never get over the phenomenon of midnight sun. We never needed an arena light, even at night shows. Finding our way to our Pullman car at midnight, we picked our way along in twilight. Once in a while, we'd come back from shopping in town to find our train gone. It seems they would move it to a different track and we'd have to hike around the railroad yards looking for home . . .

"I rode eight to ten broncs a week during all these rodeos [from 1930] until 1948." The last ride took her by surprise. "The pick up man took me off the bronc and set me down in the middle of the arena. The cowboys and cowgirls came running out to me with flowers and a silver tray. I was wondering what was going on, when Bill said to me 'Mary, that's your last bronc.' Bill had retired me."

VIVIAN WHITE
1912–

Having the distinction of winning the last female bronc riding competition held at Madison Square Garden, Vivian White began her rough stock career at age fifteen with steer riding exhibitions. A popular rider, she once rode a buffalo to the delight of fans at a local show just east of her Enid, Oklahoma, birthplace.

While completing her high school education, Vivian performed as an exhibition steer rider. She later rode saddle broncs, competing for prizes in the arena. Success followed quickly with a 1937 victory in Ladies Saddle Bronc Riding at Fort Worth, Texas, followed the next year with her first world championship. She won the trophy, saddle, and cash prize at Madison Square Garden in 1938, the same year her trick-riding secured the top prize in Cheyenne, Wyoming.

As with many riders of her time, Vivian's career waned as opportunities to compete in women's rough stock riding eroded. All girl rodeos were originally designed to entertain America's wartime troops and to give cowgirls a chance to continue their careers. They had recently been excluded from major competitions. Several shows of this kind were planned for Texas in late 1942, starring a series of Madison Square Garden veterans. Vivian was one of the featured riders in the first performance of Fay Kirkwood's all girl rodeo held at the Bonham, Texas, Fannin County Fairgrounds. Sports historians believe that despite the popularity and reported financial success of these contests, increased tire and gas rationing in the early forties forced them to fold. The all girl rodeos were a homefront casualty of World War II, but luckily resurfaced a few years later.

With the creation of the Girls Rodeo Association, Vivian resumed her competitive career. While serving as a founding board member, she earned the 1949 Texas GRA's saddle bronc championship.

A lifetime member of both the Cowboys Turtle Association and the Professional Rodeo Cowboys Association, Vivian shared her numerous talents by training other rodeo performers along with Hollywood stunt riders.

Vivian White holds a place of honor in the history of rough stock riding. Though there were other female saddle bronc champions, she is believed to be the only woman rider never bucked off her horse while competing in the rodeo arena. She always waited for the pickup man.

MARGIE GREENOUGH HENSON
1908–

I was a jockey and rode straightaway races at state and county fairs for several years," Margie Greenough remembers. "Then I started riding broncs, and that was a thrilling life."

Born on a Montana homestead, Margie's father "Packsaddle" Ben Greenough won America's first recorded bucking horse contest in 1902, and all eight of the Greenough children learned to ride and rope to help operate the family ranch. Five of the siblings spent at least part of their careers in the rodeo arena. Like many rural girls, Margie's and her riding sister Alice's formal educations ended early. They completed school through the eighth grade and then began to work, not only on the Greenough Ranch, but on area homesteads for local ranchers to bring home extra money.

In 1929 the sisters answered a *Billboard* magazine advertisement for rodeo riders and joined up with the King Brothers Wild West Rodeo and Hippodrome Racing Unit. One of the last of the big Wild West shows, King Brothers, though not considered a prestigious troupe, introduced the Greenough sisters to performing, and by the following season they were ready to launch their more lucrative competitive careers.

Also, while with the Wild West show, Margie met her husband, bulldogger, Heavy Henson. Though she married in 1930, Margie continued to rodeo and perform exhibitions, using her maiden name.

"There were dangers from the time I got on my horse in the chute until I finished the ride and was taken off . . . by the pickup man," the outstanding bronc rider remembers. "After we are out in the open, I had to take care of myself too, and at the same time remember all the things I must and must not do to make a good ride. The harder the horse bucked, the better . . . it was for me."

Margie crossed the United States and made those good rides in all but three of the states until she retired from the arena in 1954 and settled in Arizona, next door to her sister Alice.

Celebrating the family of accomplished horsemen, Red Lodge, Montana, still proudly calls itself "home of the famous riding Greenoughs." Margie's son Chuck Henson continued the family tradition and performed in professional rodeo. In 1978, he was named Professional Rodeo Cowboys Association Clown of the Year.

"Rodeo was born in us," Margie Greenough remembers. "We learned to ride horses before we could walk. Dad would give us a bucking horse and expect us to make a good horse out of him. If we got bucked off, we better find him and bring him back home."

ALICE GREENOUGH ORR
1902–

First time I rode bronc for a crowd was at Forsythe, Montana. These cowboys decided I ought to ride a bucking horse . . ." recalled Alice, daughter of Montana rancher "Packsaddle" Ben Greenough. "I didn't buck off," she added proudly. That early experience began a career colored with the twists and spills of competitive rodeo.

In 1929, Alice and her sister Margie answered an advertisement for bronc and trick riders from King's Wild West Show. "It wasn't very long 'til we got a telegram back telling us to be sure and come to meet them in Ohio," Alice reported. Following their brothers into show business, the sisters rode broncs, buffaloes, and acted in skits while gaining experience to launch their competitive careers.

In late 1929, Alice Greenough competed for the first time at Madison Square Garden. When she was hung up in the saddle at an El Paso rodeo, Alice suffered a severely broken ankle followed by a nine-month hospital stay; but with a series of pins connecting her bones, Alice returned to the premiere New York Rodeo in 1931, riding grand entry and quadrilles. Contracted to ride at the country's popular bullfights during her 1933 trip to Spain, Alice did not find the steers she was accustomed to riding in American rodeos. So, she traveled the country exhibiting her skills on sleek black bulls and performing horseback stunts.

"I won Boston Yard in thirty-three, thirty-five, and thirty-six . . . I went to Australia in thirty-four . . . I won their international buck-jumping contest. I went back in thirty-nine." A popular figure, Alice endorsed a number of Australian products and after her Madison Square Garden win, signed American advertising contracts as well.

"Forty-one was the last year they had girl's bronc riding in New York . . . so I went into the rodeo business with my old friend Joe Orr," Alice explained. Starting as stock contractors, the Greenough-Orr Rodeo Company produced Northwest competitions through 1959. Alice kept the books, hired entertainment, and gave bronc riding exhibitions. The couple later married and settled in Arizona.

During her marriage, Alice Greenough managed a veterinary supply store and, after Joe's death, operated a livestock exchange restaurant together with riding sister and next-door neighbor Margie.

Alice, who once taught Dale Evans to ride, has acted and driven wagons in westerns filmed near her Arizona home. "It's hard telling how many rodeos we won," mused Alice. "We came from a great era."

ANNE SCHLEY STRADLING
1913–1992

As founder of the world's only museum dedicated to the venerable history of the horse, Anne Schley Stradling has shared her love of all things western with thousands of tourists.

Born to skilled equestrians in suburban New York, Anne's first equine experiences—fox hunting, polo, horse shows, and driving competitions—were far from the western stunts she performed as a show cowgirl. A visit to an uncle's ranch in Fort Garland, Colorado, changed her destiny. On that trip, Stradling decided to become a cowgirl.

While still a teenager, Anne traveled with the legendary Miller Brothers 101 Ranch Wild West Show as a trick rider, calf roper, and wrangler. After Anne married the 101's ranch manager, recognizing the public's fascination with the West, the couple bought a portion of the Oklahoma outfit, seeking to preserve elements of the historic show.

After Anne and her husband divorced, she moved to New Mexico where she met and married Floyd Stradling, whose family raised fine Quarter Horses. The newlyweds made Patagonia, Arizona, their home.

Initial museum exhibits, housed at the original Patagonia location, featured family collections that were quickly expanded as Anne bought Indian relics, all types of tack, wagons, and a variety of items the museum's original benefactor considered valuable in presenting the past to visitors. She bought important collections of saddles, art, and guns.

Anne Stradling's Museum of the Horse boasts original art by western masters Remington and Russell in addition to a copy of photographer Edward Curtis' *History of the American Indian*, a historic volume documenting America's Indian tribes and people.

When arthritis forced her retirement from ranching and riding, Anne continued to work for and financially support her museum honoring one of man's most important gifts from the animal world. Faced with her own death, Anne was determined to find a new home for the collection where all her treasures would remain intact. In late 1992 The Anne C. Stradling Museum of the Horse opened in Ruidoso Downs, New Mexico, supported by the Hubbard Foundation. Stradling's collection has grown from a one-room exhibit in 1960 to its present 60,000-square-foot custom-built location. Anne was perhaps best described by her close friend, Doris Seibold, as ". . . a preserver of all things western, it's the horse that her life has been dedicated to. Anne is a true western spirit."

Marjorie Roberts Hart
1916–1982

The eldest of six children, Marjorie Roberts Hart led her family to rodeo. Though her brothers Ken and Gerald are named in the National Cowboy Hall of Fame and her father was 1979's Rodeo Man of the Year, she was the first child of E. C. Roberts to work in the arena. Marjorie, a bronc, steer, and trick rider, turned the lessons she learned in the family horse-breaking business into arena success.

Already an accomplished rider at sixteen with the experience of many amateur and pasture rodeos behind her, Margie hitchhiked to Sydney, Iowa, and found work as a ten-dollar-a-week bronc and quadrille rider with the Clyde S. Miller Society Horse Show and Rodeo and Wild West Troupe. Her early career nearly derailed when Mrs. Miller discovered her age; Margie was able to secure her parents' permission to perform, providing she returned each fall to finish high school. While touring with Miller's show, wonderful training for the young cowgirl, she learned trick and fancy riding, as well as finer points of dressage.

With a few secure trick riding contracts, Margie joined the competitive rodeo circuit in 1937. Riding steers and broncs at major rodeos from Pendleton to Houston, her greatest rough stock success came in 1941 as she captured the ladies bronc riding title at Cheyenne Frontier Days.

Only a few years before, such a feat would have made her a superstar at Boston and Madison Square gardens, but opportunities for women's competition no longer existed in those popular sites.

Although she continued to compete in available contests, including Vaughn Krieg's Flying V All Cowgirl Rodeo of 1942, Marjorie perhaps achieved her greatest rodeo fame as a thrilling and courageous contract trick rider. She performed the "dive" for rodeo audiences, a hazardous stunt demanding the rider stand in straps to lean out straight and stiff with arms raised aloft over a running horse's neck.

Wintering in Arizona and guiding trail rides for dude ranches led Marjorie, with her father's assistance, to manage the riding concession at Ozark State Park in Missouri.

Later, with her husband, Al Hart, Margie operated a cattle-breeding operation near her childhood home of Strong City, Kansas.

Fortunate enough to have experienced many areas of cowgirl life, Marjorie Roberts Hart ended her days creating gentle oil paintings of western scenes, concentrating most on her native Flint Hills. A special exhibition of her work was held at the 1986 Flint Hills Rodeo in Strong City, another success for a rodeo champion.

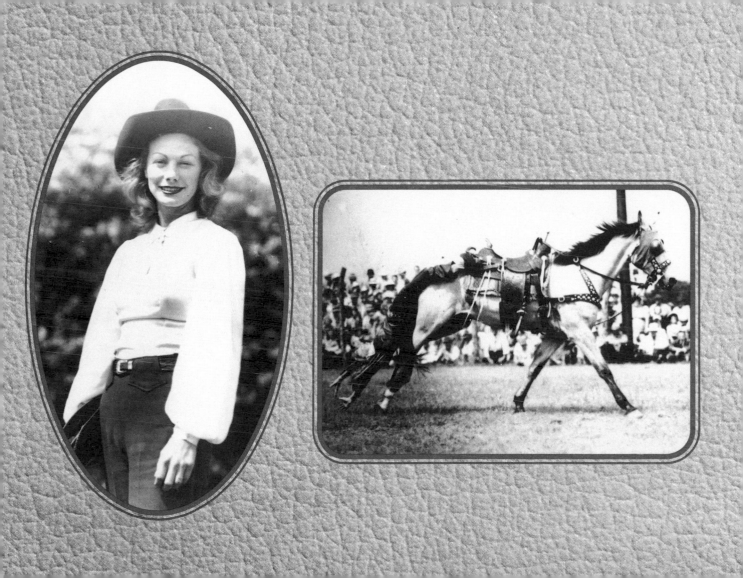

JUANITA HOWELL
1910–

Separated from her mother at age five, Juanita Howell nevertheless followed her to a circus career. Billed as "Prairie Fawn," Juanita's mother, Kathleen, rode saddle broncs and performed Indian ceremonial dances and rode for horse roping stunts. Juanita left her unhappy marriage, and together she and her mother stitched extravagant costumes for a 1932 tour with the King Brothers Circus.

Juanita managed the trained goat act, stood for bullwhip demonstrations, and later rode in the cowgirl races and horse catches. She concentrated on trick riding skills while the show wintered in Ohio. When Kathleen's career was stalled by a broken wrist, Juanita made her trick riding debut at Boston Garden in 1933.

A 1935 contract with the Boren Rodeo took the young trick rider to the Tex Austin Rodeo at Gilmore Stadium in Los Angeles, where Will Rogers made his last rodeo appearance and Juanita first met Chet Howell, who had just signed for a Japanese tour. "Art Boden offered me a contract . . . ," Juanita remembers. "I agreed to go if mother would also get a contract . . . however, my mother advised she was getting married and quitting show business, so I canceled my contract and stayed on with the Boren outfit."

After the Japanese tour, Chet found reasons to follow Juanita's show, and the couple decided to make a team. On August 9, 1936, their horseback wedding was a featured attraction at the evening performance in Centralia, Washington. Showman Montie Montana and wife, Louise, saddled up as best man and matron of honor.

"By spring of 1938 we were ready to rodeo," Juanita recalls. Starting out on their own instead of part of a traveling troupe, Chet bought their horses, and Juanita fashioned the elaborate his-and-her costumes for which she was well known. She was, in fact, once approached by a famous western rodeo tailor to design for his company.

Energetically promoting their act, the Howells enjoyed several busy seasons until wartime tire and gasoline rationing made travel difficult. Chet was drafted in 1944, but after World War II the couple resumed their career on the traveling specialty act/rodeo circuit.

"We both trick ride and spin ropes, and Chet makes horse catches," one of Juanita's promotional letters read. "Our horses run fast at all times and are always immaculately white and decked out in silver-mounted equipment. We do top tricks, and our wardrobe is surpassed by NONE."

BERNICE LUCILLE HOPPE DEAN
1915–1980

Bernice Hoppe lugged her saddle across the fairgrounds parking lot in San Jose, California. When an interested cowboy caught up to her and offered help, eighteen-year-old Bernice took her first good look at future husband Frank Dean and responded, "Okay."

Little time passed before Bernice followed up their meeting with a phone call, asking Frank to shoe her horse. The cowboy dropped everything to drive his 1932 Dodge to her home in Palo Alto. When the job was finished, Bernice rewarded him with a plate of her hot apple pie, testing the old adage for the way to a man's heart.

A versatile showman, Frank had earned a career in rodeo and Wild West shows, but a scheduled Japanese tour caused him to worry about leaving Bernice. His solution was getting her a job with the show as a trick rider. Bernice knew nothing of Frank's scheme and didn't even know how to trick ride. When she got the job, the two trained day and night, knowing the tougher job would be winning her mother's approval, but the show's assurance of a chaperone settled that matter.

In Japan, Frank and Bernice were married on horseback at the United States Consulate. The partners for life also became partners in show biz. Bernice rode for Frank's horse roping stunts, stood for his knife throwing feat, and popped whips with him in their Australian bullwhip exhibitions. In the shooting act, she expertly aimed her .22 rifle at an aspirin twenty feet away.

With nerves of steel, Bernice never flinched as Frank's knives outlined her figure, the daggers bounding her so closely, she couldn't step away until they'd been removed. Sometimes the pointed blades pinned her clothes to the wall. A cigarette was boldly held between her lips until the pop of Frank's whip sliced it in two, and she posed motionless as he adeptly shot balloons from her shoulders.

More than an assistant to Frank, Bernice developed her own expertise, throwing knives, making ocean wave catches with the difficult Mexican maguey rope, and juggling while balancing on the rolling globe or rola-rola. She exhibited rare ability on a horse with the backwards Hippodrome Stand, popping her bullwhip simultaneously.

September 8, 1938, in Filer, Idaho, Bernice rode against legendary track star Jesse Owens in his triumphant foot race—a historic moment with the "world's fastest human" of that time.

Bernice and Frank's forty-five-year career included movie parts with Roy Rogers and in the film *The Great Ziegfeld*. They took in every state and Canada and spanned five countries of East Asia.

DIXIE LEE REGER MOSLEY
1930–

Literally born into rodeo, Dixie Lee Reger Mosley toured with her family and a trained longhorn named Bobby Twister, and at five she made her solo debut as part of J. E. Eskew's L. E. Ranch Rodeo, trick riding on a sturdy, lovable Shetland pony.

Well known on the rodeo circuit, the Reger family troupe toured with Eskew's Ranch Rodeo, and later Dixie's father—announcer, producer, and contract performer Monte Reger—formed his own show with the children trick riding, roping, and demonstrating dangerous and popular horseback jumps. Before Dixie's teens the family had toured every state in the union. The young star completed elementary school through correspondence.

At eleven years old, already a seasoned veteran of the traveling rodeo circuit, Dixie secured her place in the sport's colorful history. She was one of the first female rodeo clowns. More than a sideshow, rodeo clowns take center stage, keeping the audiences interested during the often difficult and sometimes lengthy changeover of events. "Believe me," Dixie said, "a two-hour show is hard work."

An early newspaper account reported, "Throughout the show, Little Dixie Lee Reger . . . kept the crowd amused . . . At one point she trapped one man in the stands and kissed him."

During this time, the family settled in Oklahoma, their first actual home. Despite a full-time rodeo career, Dixie attended high school and with her mother's tutoring managed to graduate at fifteen.

In 1947, the family contracted to work Nancy Binford and Thena Mae Farr's Tri-State All Girl Rodeo. Dixie, excited by the opportunities offered women by all girl competition, not only clowned the entire show, but also entered seven of the events offered, including bronc, bull and trick riding, calf and ribbon roping, barrel racing, and the wild Brahma scramble. Though the landmark Amarillo contest was Dixie's first competitive experience, she placed in three events and ended in the finals of two others. "We girls sure wanted to put the show over and entered as many events as we could," Dixie explained.

Dixie and the Reger family continued to perform at many of Binford and Farr's events, and to this day Nancy Binford believes the Regers were instrumental in the Tri-State All Girl Rodeo's success. Dixie devoted the remainder of her career to all girl events, serving as GRA Contract Representative and vice president from 1950 to 1952.

Dixie retired from professional rodeo upon her 1953 marriage to William C. Mosley. The bride wore cowboy boots.

DOROTHY TOMLINSON SATTERFIELD
1924–

Although Dorothy Satterfield and her paint gelding Lucky first became known to rodeo fans in the mid-forties, this self-taught rider had her start at the tender age of twelve as the *Denver Post*'s Best Cowgirl contest winner, awarded at the National Western Stock Show.

The prize, a flash pinto mare, gave birth to more than Dorothy's trick riding partner; she also gave birth to a career in which Dorothy entertained audiences, won prize money in the contest of barrel racing, and rode with great success in the American Quarter Horse Association show ring.

Dorothy describes those years as learning by "trial and error." That ongoing education and the support of her family helped Dorothy train Lucky and begin her performing career at the 1944 Greeley Independence Stampede. A crowd-pleasing exhibition brought her offers from rodeo producers across the West. Traveling with her mother and sporting show outfits her mother handstitched, Dorothy found love on the road.

A bulldogger and rough stock rider, Carl Satterfield, became the Wyoming trick rider's traveling companion. After his young wife volunteered him to a show committee in need of a bullfighter, Carl and Dorothy Satterfield started to take home two sure paychecks from every rodeo performance. In a sport where horses are athletes equal to the rider, Dorothy's extraordinary equine skills allowed her to compete and win, often on borrowed mounts.

For more than a decade the lady who could train horses, perform thrilling tricks, fearlessly race against formidable competitors, or ride quadrille in perfect time made rodeo her life, often serving as rodeo secretary and timer in addition to being a popular rider.

When they retired from rodeo in 1956, Dorothy and Carl devoted full attention to training and showing the recently organized Quarter Horse breed. As a team, they have been rewarded with four AQHA champions among other honors. A move to Tucson in 1969 saw the creation of a successful breeding program. Dorothy, ever the willing showwoman, with husband, Carl, has trained and ridden Satterfield horses to high praise in a variety of performance classes.

Of her two children, Satterfield's daughter carries on the family tradition of horsemanship and performance. Like her mother, Dorothy explains, "Carla . . . breeds, trains, rides, and shows horses . . ."

"I've been around and on horses all my life," PRCA gold-card holder Dorothy Satterfield remembers happily. ". . . We'll always want to keep a couple good ones around."

FAYE BLACKSTONE
1915–

As an excited high school graduate, Faye Blackstone, one of America's outstanding trick and fancy riders, chose her profession while sitting in the stands with her uncle at a local rodeo. Faye determined her future career as she watched rodeo legend Mabel Strickland perform.

While competing locally in her native Nebraska at one of her early contests, the young rider met Texas cowhand and international rodeo circuit rider Vick Blackstone. As man and wife, the couple traveled the rodeo circuit full-time from 1937 to 1951, performing and competing at all the major contests of the day in Mexico, Hawaii, Canada, Texas, and Madison Square Garden, among other popular locations.

A fearless rider, Faye invented the dangerous "Reverse Fender Drag." The stunt was featured in her performances, and its popularity led to bookings at big rodeos across the Northwest and, in fact, around the world. In 1951, the rodeo couple worked an international event in Havana, Cuba. Faye thrilled the crowd with twenty-two contract trick riding performances over the sixteen-day-long competition.

For her fellow performers, Faye Blackstone personally trained a series of fourteen horses. Though she believes geldings to be the best in the arena, her favorite was a talented mare she called Cricket.

She was most revered for her death-defying stunts performed with seemingly reckless abandon and natural grace. When opportunities for women in the rough stock and trick riding arenas began to falter (nearly coinciding with the beginning of World War II), Faye Blackstone began what amounted to a second riding career, often finishing in the prize money on the flag and, later, barrel racing circuits.

The Madison Square Garden Rodeo discontinued the cowgirl bronc riding after the 1941 performance, and many of Faye's cowgirl contemporaries chose not to compete in what they considered tamer events. Yet, the former trick rider's love of horses and riding continued to carry her down the road to the next rodeo and any contest then available.

After more than 30,000 miles on the road and making a home in trailers and tents, Vick and Faye settled in Florida, where they had wintered during their rodeo years. Though Vick passed away in 1987, Faye continues to ride every day and is an active member of the Florida Cowbelles Association.

One of the last great fancy and trick riding artists, Faye Blackstone, highly regarded for her skill and courage, was honored by the National Cowgirl Hall of Fame in 1982 for her contribution to a part of rodeo that all but vanished from the arena.

NANCY KELLY SHEPPARD
1929–

Nancy Kelley Sheppard was born December 29, 1929, to fourth-generation Texas cattle ranchers. Inspired as the granddaughter of a skilled roper and daughter of a professional rodeo cowboy and accomplished maguey roper, she made her first professional appearance at age nine at the Rowell Ranch Rodeo in Hayward, California.

Nancy's parents later separated when she was twelve, but her career was taken under the wing of rodeo producer Everett E. Colburn of the Lightning C Ranch in Dublin, Texas. Nancy continued honing her abilities with the study of acrobatics, tumbling, trapeze, tap, and folk dancing. By age seventeen, she arrived at the prestigious Madison Square Garden in New York.

Nancy performed quadrilles, trick riding, and roping, as well as worked promotional acts for the major rodeo producers between 1939 and 1961. She visited hospitals with other rodeo personalities wherever she was performing and had a New York fan club. Nancy was also roped in for appearances on the national television shows "What's My Line?" and "The Arthur Godfrey Show."

Along with modeling jobs, Nancy was a consultant for major western-wear firms and chose the colors for Lee Rider's first departure from blue denim. Tony Lama boots featured her in full-page, full-color ads. In 1953, Hollywood's Republic Studios offered her a leading role, but Nancy declined, saying, "I'd rather play to a live audience where I can hear the applause."

In the 1950s, Nancy was elected Contract Spokeswoman for the Rodeo Cowboys Association. Her own contracted skills included the hippodrome stand, Nancy's specialty, executed at a run while spinning a loop in each hand.

The cowgirl's first "settled existence" was the gift of a move in 1946 to Globe, Arizona, with her mother. She spent the mild winter months training her horses and designing stunning costumes.

In Globe, Nancy met professional calf roper Lynn Sheppard. They married in 1948 and took to the road together, with Nancy giving the next two winters to working as a pony girl and the hazardous outrider job at the Rillito Race Track in Tucson, Arizona.

Some years later, at the age of forty, Nancy earned her G.E.D. certificate, a credit long delayed because of Nancy dropping out of high school following her sophomore year in order to work and help support her mother.

Nancy still leans to helping. Between ranch responsibilities, she fits in time assisting young people eager to ride, rope, and train horses.

MARGARET OWENS MONTGOMERY
1922–1955

From roundups and brandings on her family's Texas ranch, to breaking and training her own horses, Margaret Owens Montgomery showed exceptional talent at a remarkably young age.

Because her first rodeo in her hometown of Ozona, Texas, had no women's competition, Margaret competed against the men in the breakaway roping. Future competitions against men, and later women contestants, brought success and a series of trophy saddles, buckles, and prize money.

Known as an outstanding roper, perhaps this early competitor's most notable achievement was her tenure as first president and founding member of the Girls Rodeo Association. Organized in 1948, the GRA set standards for the first time in women's competition both in all girl and Rodeo Cowboys Association events.

That founding year, Margaret Montgomery was the association's first world champion all-around cowgirl and also won the 1948 titles in the barrel, flag racing, and cutting. In 1949, she added to her honors by winning the wild cow milking world championship, placing second in calf roping and claiming bareback riding's third-place finish. In her first four years of GRA competition, Montgomery won thirteen buckles and five saddles at association-sanctioned events.

Early in her career Margaret won the 1940 Fort Worth Ranch Girl sponsor contest. These contests, which had often been judged more on the rider's beauty and costume than her athletic ability, in 1939 joined the programs of major Texas rodeos, where competition was more legitimate. The GRA helped bring these early contests, often decided by somewhat arbitrary standards, to a halt. The association replaced these rivalries with standard timed events and rules based on the system established by the men's RCA. Sponsor contests, many believe, evolved into today's rodeo queen competitions. Influenced by the newly formed GRA, barrel racing became the women's event at small local rodeos and in 1954 made its Madison Square Garden debut.

The GRA, known today as the Women's Professional Rodeo Association (WPRA), was founded by Margaret and a group of her fellow women riders in February 1948. It is the oldest organization of professional female athletes in America and the only such group managed entirely by women.

After her divorce from calf roper and rancher Vic Montgomery, Margaret operated a ranch near Rankin, Texas, and continued to compete until an automobile accident claimed her life in 1955. Dead at thirty-three, Margaret Owens Montgomery helped pave the way for today's women competitors and has earned a place in the history of the sport.

NANCY BINFORD
1921–

Despite her winning competitive record, Nancy Binford is best remembered as a talented producer who created opportunities for other rodeo women. In 1947 Nancy, along with coproducer Thena Mae Farr, created, organized, and promoted the Tri-State All Girls Rodeo, drawing large crowds with sizable prizes for women.

A noted beauty, in 1939 Nancy was chosen Sweetheart of the Range Riders Club of Amarillo. She traveled to horse shows and rodeos with the group, learning valuable lessons in public relations. In 1947, as the Hereford, Texas, contestant, Nancy, one of the few college graduates on the rodeo circuit, was crowned queen of the All-American Rodeo and Horse Show in Fort Worth, which tempted cowgirls with exceptional prize money. A Cowboy Turtles Association strike closed the event and caused its bankruptcy. Nancy competed in calf roping, but no prize money was awarded.

Despite a series of wins in sponsor contests, Nancy and Thena Mae were reportedly dissatisfied with the state of women's competition. They convinced Amarillo's Tri-State Fair, badly in need of quality entertainment, to try their All Girl Rodeo.

Nancy and Thena Mae, with the help of Nancy's sister Barbara, sold program advertisements, arranged for prizes, and attracted a field of seventy-five female competitors, including top cowgirl Jackie Worthington and cutting star Fern Sawyer. Cowgirls rode for prize money in bareback, calf roping, barrel racing, cutting, and team tying. The saddle bronc and steer riding exhibitions awarded mount money, and because it only attracted one entry, bulldogging was performed as an exhibition by lone contestant Pat McClain.

The 1947 rodeo attracted the biggest crowd in the fairground's history. Local media called it a "knockout." Nancy and Thena Mae continued to produce popular all girl rodeos until 1951, when both women returned to competitive rodeo.

Highly regarded for her skills with cattle and horses, which she learned by age thirteen while helping her mother manage the family ranch, Nancy was the only woman selected by the American Quarter Horse Association to ride in the 1948 Chicago Cutting Exhibition.

Instrumental in forming the GRA, Nancy, who served as the association's 1950 president, retired from the arena five years later. Nancy Binford has managed the family horse, cow-calf, and farm operations on the family ranch, but she will always be remembered for her tireless dedication to the cause of promoting women's rodeo.

Today's women riders may owe their chance to compete to Nancy, Thena Mae, and the women of the GRA—who secured a future for women's events.

FERN SAWYER
1917–1993

I was on a horse from morning 'til night, growing up. Daddy always told me, '. . . you can either help me, or you can go help your mother in the house. That's your choice. But if you go with us, you are going to be treated just like one of the cowboys. You don't quit.' "

All too aware of the horse fever galloping in her veins, Fern resolutely turned her back on the bland appeal of house chores to earn the prized distinction of top hand on her family's ranch. "I know I have the respect of all the cowmen and all the cowboys; I always have had—'cause I work good as they do."

Horse fever naturally turned to rodeo fever, and a stellar career was launched with a win in Lovington, New Mexico's sponsor contest, when Fern was fifteen. "I knew how to ride a horse and I wanted to prove to the world I could." Haunting every rodeo she could find, Fern frequently competed in men's events, finding the women's offerings too uninspiring and infrequent for her competitive zeal. She collected barrel racing trophy saddles for every month of the year, but preferred those events that worked the stock.

In 1945, Fern claimed the esteem of generations of cowmen when she became the only woman to win the National Cutting Horse world title at the Fort Worth Fat Stock Show and Rodeo, outshining a field of around 150 leading male equestrians. The accomplishment secured her singular female place in the Cutting Horse Hall of Fame.

At a breakthrough production of the 1947 Tri-State All Girl Rodeo in Amarillo, Texas, Fern competed in tag races, cutting, barrel racing, calf roping, and team roping. "It was the best rodeo we ever had," Fern recalled. " 'Cause, first place, they got too rough of stock . . . like to killed us all." Then Fern was asked to ride the bulls "because most all the girls had their legs broke, and arms . . . But, my dad, he just wouldn't let me ride bulls." This time Fern was determined, "I just went anyway."

Peering through the fence, Mr. Sawyer relented, "Well, if you get on him, you damn sure better ride him." Fern did. She gripped so hard, her hand broke in nine places, but she carried off the title of Best All-Around Cowgirl.

MARY ELLEN "DUDE" BARTON
1924–

Born into a family of Texas ranching pioneers, Dude Barton as a baby was rocked to sleep on the back of her father's gentle plowhorse.

At fifteen, Dude entered her first competition in nearby Matador, Texas. Early in her tremendously winning career, she out-roped Madison Square Garden's veteran Sydna Yokley, claimed the balloon race and a sponsor contest's prizes at the Old Settler's Reunion, and won four timed events before a Floydada, Texas, crowd of twelve thousand.

Early sponsor contests were routinely decided by arbitrary standards and a flexible set of rules, but starting in 1939 and during the time Dude Barton competed, they had arrived as mostly honest contests, garnered, at least in part, by athletic prowess. They were frequently the only events open to women.

In 1942, after collecting two saddles, spurs, and $250 from local competitions, Dude was invited to Fort Worth's Fat Stock Show and carried off the sponsor's musical chairs prize by winning eight of the nineteen segments of that event's competition. At Fay Kirkwood's second all girl rodeo in Wichita Falls, Dude added to her trophy saddle collection and placed in the money in calf roping and reining, with first-place prizes in the musical chairs, flag race, and cutting horse contests.

Later that same year, Dude Barton accomplished her most famous win. She handily defeated a field of fifty-six male contestants to win the ribbon roping at the Motley-Dickens Counties Old Settler's Reunion.

The historic Tri-State All Girl Rodeo in 1947 brought another sponsor contest win and a first in calf roping against a field of highly regarded, talented riders. At Midland later that year, Dude, who at two years old rode nimbly behind her father on his swiftest ranch horse, became the first entrant to win both the sponsor and the cowgirl's cutting horse contests.

Before retiring from the rodeo circuit, Barton served the newly formed GRA as founding vice president. Since her father's death in 1965, Dude has managed the family ranch with her lifelong friend Viola Stinson. Together the ranch women have bred and shown fine Quarter Horses and dabbled in racing.

While so young that she was tied to the saddle to protect her from a fall, Mary Ellen Barton helped drive the family herd from Flomot to Matador, Texas. As an adult, she still works the rich Texas ranchland pioneered by her grandparents in the mid-1800s, when the country was young and wild.

TEXAS ROSE BASCOM
1922–1993

Texas Rose Bascom, known as "Queen of the Trick Ropers," saw the world while introducing new fans to the cowgirl art of trick and fancy roping. Her act was billed as "The Most Beautiful Stage Performance in the World."

A popular contract performer who traveled the rodeo circuit with her husband, rodeo cowboy Weldon Bascom, Texas Rose packed her ropes and headed for Hollywood. The talented rope spinner starred and performed her popular tricks in several movies, including *The Lawless Rider*, *Smokey River Serenade*, and *The Time, The Place, and The Girl*.

In addition to roles in films, Rose performed on early television. She was a regular guest on a daytime talk show teaching her tricks, and also spent one season with the Wild Bill Elliott Show. During World War II, Rose joined the USO and entertained American servicemen at military bases and hospitals across the United States.

After the war, Rose twirled her famous lariats on a thirteen-week tour of the Philippines, Hong Kong, Tokyo, and Alaska. She traveled through Europe with the "Tex Ritter Show" and twice returned to the Far East with Johnny Grant and Bob Hope, performing for servicemen during the Christmas holidays. In appreciation for her generous efforts, General Edmund Sebree, leader of the Far East Command, presented cowgirl Texas Rose Bascom with a gold ring, a token of the servicemen's esteem, at a banquet staged in Tokyo for the entertainers and military commanders.

As popular at home as she was overseas, Rose performed twice at the famous Hollywood Bowl. Exuberantly roping all the way, hailed as "Cowgirl Queen of Las Vegas," Rose represented the desert city on a float in the annual Pasadena Rose Bowl Parade.

Of her lengthy list of accomplishments, Rose is most proud of the time she has donated entertaining for charity. For nearly two decades, Rose, with twirling fringe and soaring loops, delighted audiences to benefit the Kennedy Foundation and the Boys' Club along with a host of other worthwhile organizations. These performances teamed the talented spinner with the greatest western stars of the day: Roy Rogers, Dale Evans, Gabby Hayes, Hoot Gibson, Monty Montana, and the Sons of the Pioneers.

Texas Rose Bascom, roping star of stage, arena, and screen, enjoyed a career other performers dream about.

JACKIE WORTHINGTON
1925–1987

Jackie Worthington was the third woman to be inducted into the National Cowgirl Hall of Fame and Western Heritage Center in May 1975. She was born and raised on the West Fork Ranch in Texas. Her life justly personifies the western woman in all respects. As a child, she was literally "raised in the saddle" and early on she began rodeoing. Following her many years on the rodeo circuit (1940–1956), she returned to the West Fork where she raised Angus cattle and Angus Limousine Cross cattle.

In the rodeo arena, Jackie was a fierce and winning competitor in all events, though she was just a petite four-feet, eight-inches tall. She was the Girls Rodeo Association Champion All-Around Cowgirl for six years and held seventeen other individual world titles. She worked every event, both timed and riding. Jackie won three bareback bronc riding world championships, seven bull riding world championships, the ribbon roping world championship once, and the GRA World Championship Cutting Horse Rider six times. That totals an amazing twenty-three world championships.

Jackie also won the bull riding at the first competitive all girl rodeo, which was held in conjunction with the Tri-State Fair in Amarillo, Texas, September 1947. This rodeo led to the forming of the Girls Rodeo Association the following February. She served as president of the GRA for two terms in 1955 and 1956. She helped in planning and forming the GRA in 1948 and served as the first director of bareback bronc riding.

Jackie Worthington died September 26, 1987, at her 6,000-acre West Fork Ranch in Jack County, Texas. She was 63. As Chuck DeHaan eulogized her, "Everything that Jackie Worthington did in her lifetime, she did in a championship way."

THENA MAE FARR
1927–1985

Beauty queen, gifted athlete, and sponsor contest winner, Thena Mae Farr made her greatest contribution to women's rodeo from behind the chutes, as coproducer of the historic Tri-State All Girl Rodeo.

Though there were a few all female events before the 1947 meet, Thena Mae along with her partner Nancy Binford created a contest unique in the history of women's athletics. Not only were all the participants women, but the great majority of the arena jobs were also performed by cowgirls. The only men involved in Nancy and Thena Mae's historic Amarillo contest were the announcer Monte Reger, patriarch of the performing rodeo family, I. W. Young, a contestant's husband who manned the chutes, and the cutting competition judges.

Banking on the media savvy they learned as beauty queens, Nancy with Thena Mae—who was four times elected Miss Seymour, Texas—attracted the attention of the press, and the Tri-State All Girl Rodeo benefited from outstanding publicity. The two producers were photographed at various Amarillo locations, and popular rider Jackie Worthington delighted the press by flying to the contest in her private plane. The local papers promised rodeo fans "super chills and spills," and Nancy and Thena Mae's first event played to sellout crowds.

Encouraged by their success, Thena Mae and Nancy incorporated the Tri-State All Girl Rodeo and planned a series of contests with women both competing and performing the majority of arena jobs. San Angelo and Seymour, Texas, and Colorado Springs, Colorado, were a few of the locations where audiences cheered the women producers' historic company. Each rodeo offered substantial prize or mount money in rough stock and timed events and awarded a horse trailer to the all-around cowgirl.

Their success bred imitation, and several male producers operated similar contests. Twenty-four all girl rodeos sprang up in 1950 alone. Without Nancy and Thena Mae, who ceased operations in 1951, all female rodeos stopped growing in the mid-fifties, never topping thirty contests a year. In 1993, thirteen of the events were governed by the PWRA, a division of the Women's Professional Rodeo Association.

Thena Mae Farr went on to serve as president of the GRA, succeeding her partner Nancy Binford, and retired from competition in 1954. Like Nancy, Thena Mae Farr returned to work her family ranch after making rodeo history.

Thena Mae Farr and Nancy Binford may have been the only women to produce women's events, organized and supported by women workers—an all-too-rare occurrence in the history of women's sport.

FAYE JOHNSON BLESING
1920–

A respected horsewoman, Faye Johnson Blesing traveled the United States from her native California to New York's Madison Square Garden, performing for rodeo fans and promoting the sport she loved.

Featured at events throughout the West, Faye formed a trick riding and fancy roping act with her brothers. As an entertainer, she holds the distinction of headlining New York City's venerable rodeo for seven consecutive years, a rare accomplishment in a business where new talent is constantly surfacing and was, at the time, competing for comparatively few contract jobs.

While traveling the rodeo circuit, Faye met dashing rodeo cowboy Wag Blesing. An avid competitor, Wag covered four events at each rodeo: saddle broncs, bull riding, steer wrestling, and the relatively new sport of bareback. Reportedly taken with his lavish style and exceptional skills, after a whirlwind courtship, Faye married Wag in 1944, and the couple spent their honeymoon—where else—at the Fort Worth Fat Stock Show and Rodeo. A striking couple, Mr. and Mrs. Blesing quickly became known as "Sweethearts of the Rodeo."

A beautiful woman, always handsomely costumed, Faye performed at many rodeos produced by movie legend Gene Autry, with whom she had several film roles. At the time, Gene Autry's World Championship Rodeo company (created by the merger of Autry's Flying A and Everett Colburn's Lightning C rodeo companies) was the largest and most powerful in the sport's long history. Autry's company produced lavish patriotic programs, with parades and spectacular production numbers worthy of his Hollywood experience.

Faye Blesing's film career expanded to include roles with the "King of the Cowboys," Roy Rogers. A 1950 *Houston Chronicle* article commenting on the cowgirl's career reported that "Many of the feminine screen stars depend upon Faye to double for them and brave the dangers of fast and difficult riding and other stunts that are beyond the nerve and the ability of the high-priced girls of the Flicker Colony."

In huge demand for commercial product endorsements, Faye lent her exceptional charms to the marketing of saddles, western clothing, cigarettes, and war bonds. For many years the famous Stetson Hat Company offered hats shaped into "The Faye Blesing Crease."

"Were it not for the fact that Faye loves rodeo work far better than the make-believe acting of the silver screen," the Houston article said, "she would easily be one of the great stars of the movies."

Ruby Gobble
1930–

Ruby Gobble began cowgirling on the desert burros of her family's Arizona ranch. At age twelve, she was granted the foal of a paint mare. Ruby broke Tony to a saddle and taught him tricks. They put together a rodeo act that was in demand across the state. Tragically, a kick from another horse caused an infection, and five-year-old Tony died.

A brokenhearted Ruby was gifted by her father with a palomino pony named Taffy and bravely resumed her career. Trained within three months, Taffy entered the arena with Ruby to thrill appreciative crowds. Their repertoire quickly included trick riding, a talent noted by Monty Montana, who wanted the duo in his Wild West show. But the cowgirl preferred something more.

Ruby had long been adept with a rope, so in 1946 her interests easily turned to calf roping. She learned the art from a family friend, who was a professional roper, and picked up some tips from world champion cowboy Everett Bowman.

In 1949, Ruby's exceptional skills as a horsewoman won her the title Queen of the World's Championship Rodeo, in Glendale, Arizona. Her attractiveness also inspired an unofficial title, "the glamour girl of rodeoing."

The 1950 Pikes Peak rodeo included a winning calf roping entry from Ruby, who at age nineteen set her course for the professional circuit. The first year foretold future successes, when Ruby won the runner-up spot for the title World's Champion Calf Roper. In 1951, she joined the membership ranks of the Girls Rodeo Association and accepted the role of Calf Roping Director. A buckskin gelding named Sabado partnered her in claiming the 1951 and 1953 World Champion Team Tying titles and the 1952 World Champion Ribbon Roping. Ruby's style was to throw the rope slack over the horse's head, making her one of the few lady catch-loop roping artists.

After four winning years on the circuit, setting record times, Ruby saddled up with Nancy Binford, former GRA president, and worked on the Binford Ranch until 1963. For recreation, the women slipped away from the ranch to try their luck at area rodeos.

Ruby's home now is the historic Chase Ranch of Cimarron, New Mexico, where she assists owner Gretchen Sammis as ranch foreman. The ranch's operations demand versatility from the women who run it. Ruby applies her talents, constructing sheer mountain roads, operating heavy machinery, tending to mechanical repairs and welding, performing veterinary duties, and handling major carpentry projects, besides managing livestock.

WILMA GUNN STANDARD TATE
1923–

Gunn was Texas-born and spent her first thirteen years "riding every horse I could." Moving to California in 1937, she saw her first calf roping. "The first time I saw a calf roped, I was so fascinated that I just knew I had to be a calf roper."

Without calves available for practice, Wilma learned to rope by renting a burro from the stable for fifty cents a day. Chasing it around on horseback, she roped until the burro tired of the game. "Then I'd take it back and get another one."

Wilma went to work in a restaurant to finance the purchase of her first horse, eventually selling it to buy a green colt. She broke and trained the colt for roping, bulldogging, picking up riders, jumping, and cutting.

In 1945, she saw her first rodeo. "But I saw it from a little different point of view than most people, though. I rode in it, and I won the calf roping event." Her first year of competition, Wilma placed in all twenty contests, chalking up sixteen "firsts," three "seconds," and one "third." She soon became known as "the Texas Tomboy."

Wilma's most popular feat was a personal style of Roman riding. An act usually performed with two horses, Wilma doubled up on horsepower. With four mounts side by side, she clenched their reins and, standing up, straddled them by positioning her feet on the backs of the outside pair. Just to make the act interesting, she included a series of three-feet jumps and even jumped automobiles. The act followed through with the release of three of the mounts one by one, while Wilma stood tall on remaining team members.

In 1947, Wilma coproduced several exhibition all girl rodeos in southern California. Without the benefit of an arena, the broncs were blindfolded until each cowgirl was mounted. The first show was at the Sawtelle Government Hospital grounds, where hospitalized veterans nearly tore the stands down in their enthusiasm over the performances.

Wilma worked in movies and stock show events at horse shows, eventually becoming the Pacific Coast Women's Champion in the cutting event.

During her early days of rodeo, Wilma rode broncs and steers for fun in the exhibition events but stayed a fierce contender in the roping. When other cowgirls began favoring breakaway roping over the tie down event, Wilma made strong objections about altering rules to sissy-up the event. In retaliation, other contestants spoke slightingly of Wilma's "brawn," to which a reporter decidedly observed that it was "well distributed."

JERRY ANN PORTWOOD TAYLOR
1930–

I loved the big city," Jerry Portwood said, describing her experience riding in Madison Square Garden. "To this day, the bigger the city, the more I like it." At just fifteen, Jerry had been hired as one of Gene Autry's official "Ranch Girls" for the annual western event, the youngest woman ever selected for the position. So began a more than twenty-year career of participating in rodeos and western shows across the United States and Europe.

A glamour girl of the rodeo circuit, Jerry was featured as a trick rider at the Fort Worth Fat Stock Show, the Denver Stock Show, the Phoenix Rodeo, and Cheyenne Frontier Days, to mention only a few of the major rodeos where she performed as a popular contract act.

One of the highlights of Jerry's career was her performance in *Texas*, a 1952 western stage show in London, England, starring Tex Ritter and Buck Brady. Jerry performed her trick riding routine twice a day during the production's four-month engagement.

As famous for her skill as for her style, Jerry was known for her elegant wardrobe of unique western attire. Advance promotion often featured the trend-setting competitor with her white Cadillac convertible and coordinating trailer with matching plaid tops.

In the 1950s, Jerry Portwood began to compete in a different horseback event. "In those days there weren't too many cowgirls showing cutting horses," remembers Zack T. Wood, Jr., former Executive Director of the National Cutting Horse Association. "Jerry could compete and win among the very best." Against a field of talented competitors, she won the first National Cutting Horse Association Tournament of Champions, the most prestigious event of its day.

In cutting, a team of horse and rider single an animal out from the herd and remove it from the group, a feat requiring tremendous ability and concentration from both the horse and the rider. Jerry Ann Portwood and her champion gelding Kip Mac continued to show until the horse's death in 1970.

Still a glamorous presence, Jerry Ann Portwood Taylor helped to produce and promote the 1985 Miss Rodeo Texas pageant. The contest requires cowgirls to not only ride, but understand a horse's veterinary requirements and common illnesses, along with rodeo rules, events, and competitor standings. This contest appeared to have been tailor-made for Texas rancher Jerry Ann, world-renowned for her style, grace, and horsemanship.

SYDNA YOKLEY WOODYARD
?–1959

Sydna Yokley Woodyard, a native of Canadian, Texas, and the Lazy L Ranch, was truly a woman of western heritage. All of her skills with horses and cattle were traceable to a natural way of life and learning. She was especially noted for her activities as a top-notch calf roper and rider in the forties and fifties. She was at one time one of only a few calf roping women in the world. Sonny Boy was her famous trick horse. Her performances in Madison Square Garden and Boston Garden prompted *Life* magazine to publish two full pages of arena action pictures of her performances.

Such renowned writers as Ernie Pyle of World War II fame and Eleanor Roosevelt devoted full-column stories describing her beauty, petiteness, and performing ability. Sydna helped form the American Quarter Horse Association, and she became a breeder of registered Quarter Horses in southern California. She died in 1959, when her horse kicked her to death in a horse trailer while at Winslow, Arizona.

WANDA HARPER BUSH
1931–

Every morning, on the 1,200 acres the Harper family has called home for more than 150 years, Wanda Harper Bush wakes early to feed, water, and exercise the horses that are her career. She is considered one of the world's finest barrel racing horse trainers.

Wanda started roping as a child on the Texas ranch and parlayed that early talent into several junior rodeo championships. As a charter member of the Girls Rodeo Association, the young cowgirl began a phenomenal winning career that has spanned five decades. She is the proud holder of titles in calf roping, ribbon roping, cutting, flag racing, and two in barrel racing among her incredible list of more that twenty-five world championships, including eight GRA all around cowgirl titles.

In 1959, Wanda's daughter Shanna was born. That year, the Madison Square Garden Rodeo, once the pinnacle of the season, ended its historic run, and the Professional Rodeo Cowboys Association held the first National Finals Rodeo in Dallas, Texas. Despite curtailing her travel in favor of training horses at home and keeping company with her young daughter, Wanda continued to add to her impressive career totals and still qualified for barrel racing at the National Finals after that event became part of the championship competition in 1967.

While training barrel horses and conducting clinics for young talent in the sport, Wanda remained active in rodeo long after her peers had retired. A GRA board member for more than twenty years, she was again asked to serve in 1993, filling the office of Texas Circuit Director left vacant by the death of her friend Allison Powers. More than taking an administrative interest in women's rodeo, Wanda Bush competed. At sixty-one, after back surgery and a year of recovery, she entered the barrel races at the Old Fort Futurity Days in Fort Smith, Arkansas, and won the biggest purse of her long career, $28,577.88. Had she been racing in a sanctioned rodeo, her single day's winnings would have placed her in second place in the 1992 totals behind barrel racing's first million-dollar cowgirl, Charmayne James-Rodman. Her 1953 barrel racing winnings of $3,462 were greater than the totals of all the GRA world champions that year combined.

Though Wanda Bush didn't make another NFR run, she has inspired and taught winning cowgirls like Jimmie Gibbs-Munroe, Jane Mayo, and Nancy Mayes at her popular clinics and through her winning example.

DORA RHOADS WALDROP
1911–

Folks came from miles around to see me," asserts Dora Rhoads Waldrop. Weighing in at only four pounds, the child was a celebrity at birth. The same pluck that helped the tiny infant survive distinguished her barrel racing career.

"My first job, when I was three years old, was to get the milk cows in . . . [I rode] on an old horse my dad used to chase coyotes. That old horse taught me how to ride," Dora remembers of her early days on the family's Oklahoma territory homestead. "I had to ride him bareback," she continues. "My Daddy wouldn't let me use a saddle . . . he was afraid I'd get tangled up and get hurt."

In 1931, Dora married Edgar Waldrop, her high school sweetheart. Each taught school as the other finished college and started a career. Their early married life took Dora briefly away from the horses she so loves.

"When Edgar went off to the Navy during World War II, I decided I could either get a couple of evening gowns and do a lot of dancing or get a horse," Waldrop relates. "I chose the horse and I've been riding ever since." On her ranch-trained gelding, Amarillo Streak, Dora started helping friends desperate for "cow savvy help" and later tied for a barrel racing first at 1947's Tri-State All Girl Rodeo.

Throughout her career Dora rode fine horses and collected hundreds of trophies and ribbons. When a 1951 injury briefly halted her career, Dora wrote horsemanship articles for major publications. Fully recovered, she returned to her sport as a fierce competitor.

Dora celebrated her seventy-sixth birthday with a second-place showing in barrel racing at the Living Legends Rodeo in Canadian, Texas. In 1988, barred from competing because of her age despite her 1987 All-Around High Point plaque from the Texas Quarter Horse Association, Dora urged her fellow riders to write the president of the organization and "tell him how you feel about being barred from your favorite activity because you have lived over three quarters of a century . . . You are never a quitter," Dora believes, "until you quit trying."

A true ambassador of barrel racing, Dora Rhoads Waldrop has dedicated more than forty years to the sport. "The exhilaration of getting out there and doing something well on a good horse is an exuberating feeling," Dora told a reporter in 1983. "It's not the winning," she explained, "but doing something well."

ELENOR MARIE REGINI "SISSY" THURMAN
1934–1968

On October 2, 1968, an automobile accident ended the careers of two outstanding barrel racers: Anne Lewis, ten years old and a member of the pro ranks for just a year, and Sissy Thurman, who had won all of the sport's major races at some point in her more than two decades of professional racing. That year Sissy was ranked third in the world.

Despite her success, the world title eluded Sissy. Established by a point system based on the RCA, GRA standards gave cowgirls one point for each dollar won at a sanctioned event. The competitor with the highest total was crowned World Champion. The honor, originally tabulated at the last all-girl event of the year, was later decided at the National Finals Rodeo, where Sissy twice posted the fastest time.

To win the world championship, which was nearly as much a prize for endurance as for skill, top GRA cowgirls entered as many rodeos as possible to increase their chances of winning money, which added to their yearly totals. Sissy missed the title, not for lack of skill, but because she limited her travel in favor of other rodeo-inspired pursuits. She made a successful business of training barrel horses for other riders and conducted a school to teach young girls. Though schools to teach future contestants the finer points of an event are common in the rodeo business today, Sissy Thurman's school may well have been one of the first of its kind.

Recognized for her skill in the arena, Sissy is most honored and often remembered for her exceptional sportsmanship. Described as a competitor who always had the interests of the GRA at heart, she served the association as Barrel Racing Director for several seasons.

In an article written for the GRA *News* at the time of Sissy's death, fellow competitor Frances Youree, former secretary of the Girls Rodeo Association, wrote, "Sissy was one of the friendliest barrel racers who ever entered a barrel race and was always rooting for her competitors." Youree goes on to describe how Thurman would routinely offer professional advice to other racers on the circuit, at times helping those contenders to beat her times. "That," Youree concludes, "was the kind of unselfish person Sissy was."

The accident that claimed the lives of Sissy Thurman and Anne Lewis in 1968 was called "the greatest tragedy the GRA has ever known." Sissy was survived by her husband, Doug, and two daughters, Karen and Vanessa.

THE AUTHORS

Kathy Lynn Wills is a northern Colorado nonfiction writer specializing in music, the arts, cowboy culture, and the cattle industry. She is a regular contributor to both *Cowboy* and *Cowboys and Indians* magazines and is currently working on a light-hearted collection of western recipes and chuckwagon lore. In addition to her writing, Kathy is the proprietor of the Cowboy Country General Store catalogue.

Virginia Artho is Assistant Director and Director of Publications for the National Cowgirl Hall of Fame. She edits the museum's *Sidesaddle* magazine and *Big West* newsletter and currently is writing biographical volumes on Hall of Fame honorees.